SNOOPY'S
Word Book

Peanuts® characters created and drawn by Charles M. Schulz

Text by Nancy Hall

Background illustrations by Art and Kim Ellis

W9-DFR-845

A GOLDEN BOOK • NEW YORK

Western Publishing Company, Inc., Racine, Wisconsin 53404

Copyright © 1987 United Feature Syndicate, Inc. All rights reserved. Printed in the U.S.A. by Western Publishing Company, Inc. No part of this book may be reproduced or copied in any form without written permission from the publisher. GOLDEN®, GOLDEN & DESIGN®, and A GOLDEN BOOK® are trademarks of Western Publishing Company, Inc. Library of Congress Catalog Card Number: 87-80108   ISBN: 0-307-10932-1/ISBN: 0-307-60932-4 (lib. bdg.)   A B C D E F G H I J K L M

Playing at the Park

balloon

jump rope

slide

water
fountain

ice-cream
cone

sandbox

Come with me to the park,
And we'll run, jump, and hop.

kite

tree

jungle gym

string

fishing
pole

frog

pond

Then we'll fish with a pole
That has Woodstock on top.

Let's Play Baseball

lights

cap

catcher

STRIKE THREE

batter

home plate

baseball

bat

It's time for the game—
Three strikes and you're out.

As Charlie Brown knows,
That's what baseball's about.

At the Beach

lifeguard

sailboat

sandal

blanket

seashell

It's fun at the beach—
Our lifeguard is teeny.

cloud

sea gull

ocean

sand
castle

sunglasses

beach ball

shovel

pail

crab

Do you see what I see?
It's Lucy's bikini!

Snoopy's Doghouse

house

bird

daisy

doghouse

dish

book

There's no place like home—
What could be better?

Look! Peppermint Patty
Just got a letter.

Fun in the Snow

snowman

snowball

There's snow on the ground!
Let's go out and play.

snowflakes

icicle

fence

hat

skates

ice-skating rink

mittens

First we'll make snowballs—
We'll have a great day!

A Day at School

clock

calendar

map

brushes

pencil
sharpener

paints

books

globe

schoolbag

Linus likes to study
A globe or a map.

But Peppermint Patty
Would much rather nap.

Rainy-Day Fun

curtains

raindrops

mirror

telephone

crayons

checkers

It's raining outside,
So let's stay indoors.

We'll do what you like,
But let's not do chores!

Camping Out

mountains

tent

lake

deer

cooler

sleeping bag

Let's have some dinner.
Please take your pick—

smoke

log cabin

hot dogs
and
marshmallows

cup

wood

1.5 m

Hot dogs or marshmallows
Cooked on a stick.

Falling Leaves

falling
leaves

apple tree

rake

footstool

red leaves

The leaves all change color—
It happens each fall.

It's fun to pick apples,
Then play some football.

Snoopy and Spike

sun

cactus

cloud

hill

road

Spike

rabbit

Spike loves the desert,
A very hot place.